The Winter Fox

Timothy Knapman • illustrated by Rebecca Harry

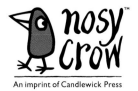

nosy crow

An imprint of Candlewick Press

Once there was a fox who played all summer long.

"Summer is nearly over!" called Fox.
"Come and play while the sun is shining!"
But his friends were all too busy.

"Winter is coming!" they said.
"We have work to do!"

The friends were worried about Fox.
What would happen to him
when winter came?

"Let me help you, Fox," said Rabbit. "I can show you **just** the right place to build a home. Then you will be near us **all** winter long."

But Fox didn't listen. He was **too busy** rolling around on the soft carpet of flowers.

So Owl tried to help.
"I can show you how to
make a cozy bed," she said.
"Then you will be snuggly
and warm all winter long."

But Fox didn't listen.

He was too busy splashing in the lake.

Next, it was Squirrel's turn to try. "I can show you how to store food," he said. "Then you will have plenty to eat **all** winter long."

But Fox **still** didn't listen. He was **too busy** chasing butterflies.

"Winter is coming," said Fox's friends. "The white snow will fall, and the freezing wind will blow. We will be tucked up till spring, but what will **you** do?"

"I will play in the snow and sing to the wind and
have the whole forest to myself!" said Fox.
"Now, come and have fun!"

But the other animals had work to do,
while Fox just played all through the autumn.

And then winter came.
The white snow fell, and
the freezing wind blew.

Rabbit had his cozy home in just the right place.

Owl had her warm and snuggly nest.

And Squirrel had lots of tasty

acorns to eat.

They were all ready for winter. But what about Fox?

Poor Fox was too cold to play
in the snow, too hungry to sing
to the wind, and he was all on
his own in the frozen forest.

Oh, I wish I'd listened
to my friends, thought Fox.

I wish, I wish . . .

Fox looked up for a star
to wish upon.

And the more he wished, the bigger the star grew.
It grew bigger and **bigger** and **bigger** until . . .

BONK!

It hit him on the head!
"Ouch!" said Fox.
But the star wasn't a star
at all! It was a box wrapped
in shiny silver paper.

Fox could have kept it
all for himself . . .

The box had broken
open, and out spilled toys
and food and bright things
that sparkled in the snow.

but he had a better idea.

Quickly, he piled everything back into the box
and set off. He had work to do!

The next morning,
Rabbit, Owl, and Squirrel
found **wonderful** gifts
outside their homes.

"Where did it all
come from?"
they wondered.

Then they spotted a trail
of paw prints in the snow
and followed them all the way to . . .

Fox! He had a great feast laid out for them.

"Presents and now this!" said the friends.
"Thank you, Fox!"

"You all tried to help me before,
but I wouldn't listen," said Fox. "I'm sorry."

When they couldn't eat anything more,
the animals played in the snow
and sang to the wind.

They chased snowflakes, went sliding across the frozen lake, and rolled on the soft carpet of snow.

At last, it started to get dark and Rabbit said, "It's nearly time for bed, Fox. Why don't you come back with us?"

So the four friends packed everything up and walked off through the forest.

As the moon rose above them,
the friends reached the big oak tree.

"See, Fox?" said Rabbit.
"If you build your home here,
you will be near us all winter long.
It's just the right place."

"And if you make a cozy bed
from this box and paper," said Owl,
"you can be snuggly and warm
when the freezing wind blows."

"And look, if you store up these leftovers,"
said Squirrel, "you will have plenty
to eat until the white snow melts."

And for once, Fox did listen.
"Thank you," he said. "You are such good friends."

Now Fox had
everything he needed.

And he was never **cold**, or **hungry**,
or **lonely** ever again.

In loving memory of my grandpa Tom Davies xxx—R. H.

To Annie, Florence, and Clementine, with love—T. K.

Text copyright © 2016 by Timothy Knapman
Illustrations copyright © 2016 by Rebecca Harry
Nosy Crow and its logos are trademarks of Nosy Crow Ltd.
Used under license.

First U.S. edition 2017

Library of Congress Catalog Card Number pending
ISBN 978-0-7636-9631-3
17 18 19 20 21 22 TEP 10 9 8 7 6 5 4 3 2 1

Printed in Panyu, Guangdong, China

This book was typeset in Bookman Old Style.
The illustrations were done using acrylic.

Nosy Crow
an imprint of
Candlewick Press
99 Dover Street
Somerville, Massachusetts 02144

www.nosycrow.com
www.candlewick.com